The zoo is built and ready now,
But so far no one's here.
No tigers or orangutans,
No skunks, but never fear:

If we sit tight and wait a bit,
I think that we might see,
The animals all traveling here
To meet with you and me!

JUDITH DREWS

THE ZOO'S
GRAND OPENING

AN ABC AND COUNTING BOOK

LITTLE
GESTALTEN

When she glided in across the rug,

Our **ANACONDA** gave me a hug.

As the first one here, I guess she's the winner,

But why does she keep on mentioning dinner?

B

Siberia is home to this big fuzzy **BEAR**,
He traveled by foot instead of by air.
The journey has left him all tuckered out,
He's going to sleep, so whisper, don't shout!

A **CHAMELEON** is hard to spot:
I can't tell whether she's here or not.
If you see her, please ask her nicely
To show us where she is, precisely.

D

Our **DROMEDARY** came from the Middle East,
He really is a magnificent beast!
His Bedouin friend walked him in with a smile,
I hope that he sticks around for a while.

E

Long trunk, two tusks and one big rear,
Our **ELEPHANT** from Kenya is here!
Everyone loves her, and so they should:
I'd be an elephant if I could.

F

This **FLAMINGO** is funny, that's what I think,
Her beak is all curved and her feathers are pink.
She often stands on one leg and not two,
I gave it a try, so now why don't you?

GIRAFFEs are tall and sort of spotty,
This one here is called Frank Biscotti.
If you want to chat, make sure you shout,
He's 20 feet from hoof to snout!

HAREs run so fast that they never grow fat:
Ours said she got here in three seconds flat.
I offered her soda and things of that ilk,
But she said she'd prefer a cold glass of milk.

If Ancient Egypt still existed,
Our **IBIS** here would still be listed
As a sacred bird that could do math,
And read and write while in the bath.

Our **JAGUAR** walked from Mexico
To ask if she could be in our show.
"Of course," I said, "I'll make you a star,"
"You won't regret having traveled so far!"

VORSICHT

K

Australia is an island way down under.
So I really have to wonder,
How strong our **KANGAROO** must be
To bring this heavy gift for me.

L

The king of the beasts just walked in through the door,
Our **LION** is regal, but boy can he roar!
I don't have a throne or a carpet that's red,
But I sure hope this crown will fit on his head.

What I wouldn't give for a mule or a moose,
A macaw or even a mini mongoose.
But the only M that has found its way here
Is a mean old **MOSQUITO** that just bit my ear!

The **NILE CROCODILE** was supposed to arrive
At a quarter past two and now it's near five.
I'm sure I could find him if I wasn't so jumpy,
But why is this ground so incredibly lumpy?

Sumatra has jungles with all sorts of trees,
They're tall and their branches sway in the breeze.
Our **ORANGUTAN** likes to climb them and dream,
Surrounded by leaves, all shiny and green.

P

Just look at that beak, what a sight to behold!
It can carry a walrus, or so I've been told.
But our **PELICAN** brought some salmon and trout,
And spat out the bones like an ill-mannered lout.

The **QUOLL** is a nocturnal chap:
When the sun is up, he likes to nap.
At night he hunts and roams around,
Australia is where he's found.

R

How would you feel if you had on your nose
A twin set of horns that you never chose?
Our **RHINOCEROS** lives like that every day,
I asked what she thought, but she chose not to say.

Our **SKUNK** might look all cute and fluffy,
But you should run like mad if he gets huffy.
A skunk that's peeved will raise its tail,
And spray a stink so bad you'll wail!

1 2 3 4 5 6 7 8 9 10 11 12 13 14 15 16 17 18 **19** 20 21 22 23 24 25 26

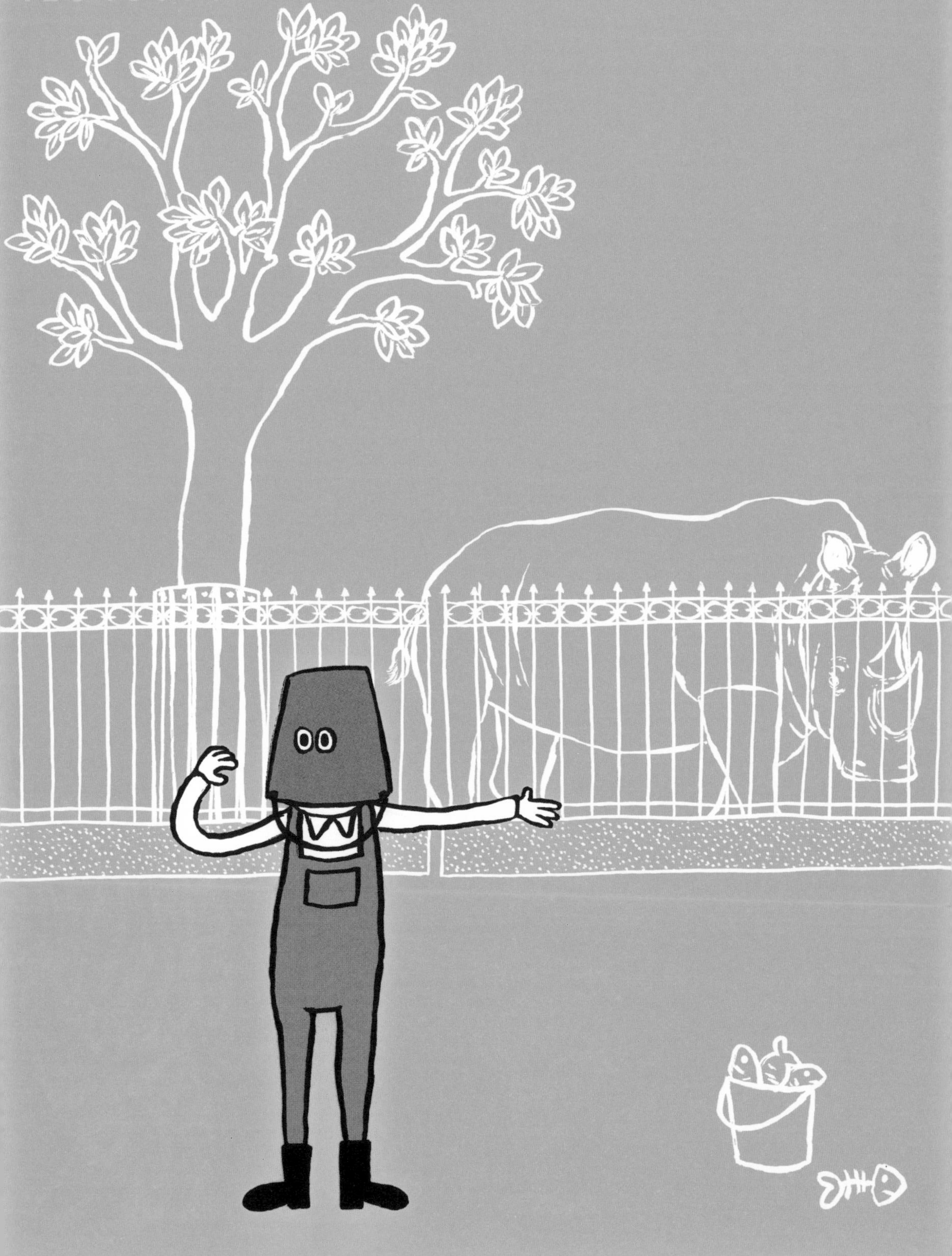

T

This **TIGER** has cool stripy fur,

A stylish beast, don't you concur?

But even though I love her look,

When I heard her growl, I shivered and shook!

A **UAKARI** is a kind of monkey,
His head is bald, his arms are chunky.
The Amazon is where he hangs out,
Swinging through trees and messing about.

V

Slithery, sneaky, hissing, and fangs,
Avoid a **VIPER** with hunger pangs!
Admire him from a long way away,
And nothing will happen to ruin your day.

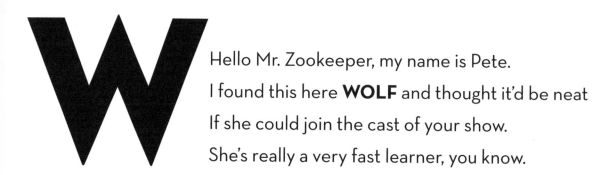

Hello Mr. Zookeeper, my name is Pete.
I found this here **WOLF** and thought it'd be neat
If she could join the cast of your show.
She's really a very fast learner, you know.

X

This **XINUSIL** martian comes from the moon,

He left in October and now we're in June.

How exciting to see a spaceship fly in,

I'd quite like to take it out for a spin!

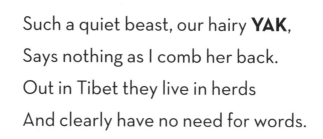

Such a quiet beast, our hairy **YAK**,
Says nothing as I comb her back.
Out in Tibet they live in herds
And clearly have no need for words.

Z

I suppose it makes sense for our ABC,
If the **ZEBRA** comes last, like a zed or a zee.
She cut it real fine but is raring to go:
Curtain up, take your seats, it's time for the show!

Ladies and gentlemen, boys and girls,
welcome to the **ZOO'S GRAND OPENING!**

The Zoo's Grand Opening

This book was conceived, edited, and designed
by Gestalten.

Edited by Hendrik Hellige and Robert Klanten
Illustrations by Judith Drews
Texts by Judith Drews and Hendrik Hellige
Translation from German by Jen Metcalf

Layout by Hendrik Hellige
Typeface: Neutra by Christian Schwartz

Printed by Livonia Print, Riga
Made in Europe

Published by Little Gestalten, Berlin 2014
ISBN: 978-3-89955-714-5

For more information, please visit www.gestalten.com.

Bibliographic information published by the Deutsche Nationalbibliothek. The
Deutsche Nationalbibliothek lists this publication in the Deutsche National-
bibliografie; detailed bibliographic data are available online at http://dnb.d-nb.de.

This book was printed on paper certified by the FSC®.

Gestalten is a climate-neutral company. We collaborate with the non-profit carbon
offset provider myclimate (http://www.myclimate.org) to neutralize the company's
carbon footprint produced through our worldwide business activities by investing
in projects that reduce CO_2 emissions (www.gestalten.com/myclimate).